Copyright © 2011 by De Vier Windstreken, Rijswijk, Netherlands.
First published in the Netherlands under the title *Kerst met Vera*.
English translation copyright © 2011 by North-South Books Inc., New York 10017.
Translated by De Vier Windstreken. Edited by Susan Pearson.
All rights reserved.
No part of this book may be reproduced or utilized in any form or by any means, electronic
or mechanical, including photo-copying, recording, or any information storage and
retrieval system, without permission in writing from the publisher.

First published in the United States, Great Britain, Canada, Australia, and New Zealand in 2011
by North-South Books Inc., an imprint of NordSüd Verlag AG, CH-8005 Zürich, Switzerland.
Distributed in the United States by North-South Books Inc., New York 10017.

Library of Congress Cataloging-in-Publication Data is available.
Printed in Belgium by Proost N.V., B 2300 Turnhout, May 2011.
ISBN: 978-0-7358-4044-7 (trade edition)
1 3 5 7 9 • 10 8 6 4 2

www.northsouth.com

FSC
www.fsc.org
MIX
Paper from
responsible sources
FSC® C101807

Marjolein Bastin

CHRISTMAS
with VERA

NorthSouth
New York / London

CONTENTS

BIANCA

Bianca is Vera's cousin from the city. She is used to the noisy, busy, exciting life of the city; and she manages to bring some of that rush and confusion along with her when she visits the Blue Cottage. She always shows up in the latest fashions—often in red, the best color for showing off her white fur.

WRENNIE

Wrennie is a house wren, always fluttering here and there on errands. But every morning she finds time to bring Vera a beautiful speckled egg.

FRITZY

Fritzy lives nearby in an abandoned nesting box, but he spends most of his time hanging around the Blue Cottage, especially when Bianca is visiting. Vera never has to look for someone to do home repairs. Fritzy is always eager to share his skill with a hammer and nails or a paintbrush.

Vera the Mouse and Her Friends

Vera

Vera lives in the Blue Cottage
with her best friends: Dolly,
Sara, Wrennie, and Ladybug.
Vera can't imagine a better
life than living in the country.
Some people think country life
is too quiet, but Vera finds plenty
to do: cleaning her house, tending
her garden, and cooking stacks
of pancakes that are piled
all the way to the ceiling.

Dolly

Dolly is Vera's
constant companion.
Such a sweet little thing—and
oh so smart for a doll! Sometimes
maybe a little too smart for her
own good? Dolly likes to think up
fun things to do—things that
often lead to mischief.

Sara

Most dogs start out as puppies, but not Sara.
She was always a funny little rag dog.
Dolly made her out of fabric scraps as a
surprise gift for Vera. Vera said that Sara
was the best gift she had ever received,
and when she hugged
the dog tightly,
she felt the soft thump of
Sara's heart. Sara came to life
because Vera loved her so much.

A White Christmas

"Shall we do a white Christmas this year?" Vera asked.

"What a strange question!" said Fritzy. "You can't order snow, can you?"

"No, silly," said Vera. "I meant that we'd decorate the Christmas tree in white this year. White and gold."

Dolly and Sara went outside to gather snowberries. Then Vera painted them gold and attached Christmas tree hooks to them. Finally Ladybug painted red stripes and stars on them.

What fun it will be when Bianca gets here. She will love the majestic Christmas tree—and especially all the golden balls.

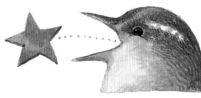

CUTTING
STAR APPLES

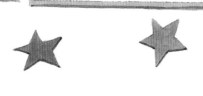

There had never been so many apples in Vera's tree.

"I know what we can do with them," said Fritzy. "But you'll have to get my pocketknife out of the cupboard."

Vera thought about that. Bianca had brought Fritzy a pocketknife from the city; but Vera thought Fritzy was too young for a pocketknife then, so she had kept it for him in the cupboard with the lock. But Fritzy was older now, and Vera was curious about what he was going to make.

"All right, Fritzy," said Vera. "But be very careful. You don't want to cut off your fingers."

Very carefully and neatly, Fritzy cut stars out of the apples.

"Now they are Star Apples," he said. "They mean that soon it will be Christmas."

"Ugh," said Ladybug. "They're turning yellow."

"That doesn't matter," said Vera. "The stars in the sky are always a bit yellow."

And what was Wrennie doing? Why, eating all the cutout stars, of course!

Do It Yourself!

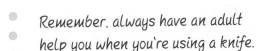

THIS IS WHAT YOU NEED:

red apples

a pencil or pen

a pocketknife

Remember, always have an adult
help you when you're using a knife.

First rinse the apples under cold water.

Rub the apples dry with a clean, soft dish towel. If you rub
them a little bit more, they will shine very nicely.

Draw the figure you want to cut out onto the apple. You can
use the star on the next page as an example.

Have an adult help you cut out the figure you have drawn
on the apple. Remember always to cut away from yourself.

After you have cut out the figures, store the apples in a cold place. If you live where it's cold, a basket on the porch or in the yard works nicely. If it's freezing outside, the apples will keep well for a long time.

Marzipan Snowballs

THIS IS WHAT YOU NEED:

½ pound blanched almonds

2 cups confectioners sugar

2 egg whites

½ tsp salt

½ tsp almond extract

more confectioners sugar

"Hey, it's snowing! Let's make snowballs!"

But Dolly didn't want cold hands.

"Then we'll make them inside," said Vera.

Vera processed the almonds, confectioners sugar, egg whites, salt, and almond extract in the food processor until everything was perfectly blended. Then she wrapped the dough in plastic wrap and put it in the refrigerator for 24 hours to harden. The next day she rolled the dough into small balls. Finally she rolled the balls in more confectioners sugar and the snowballs were ready.

Dolly's hands stayed nice and warm, and her tummy was nice and full.

A Present of
Pine Tree Branches

"Oh, Vera!" said Dolly. What a lot of pine tree branches! What on earth will you do with them all?"

"*Pffff!* I think we . . . OUCH! . . . have enough now," said Fritzy. "Mmmm. Put your nose . . . OUCH! . . . in here. It smells . . . ahhhh . . . like it's already Christmas!"

That night Vera was very busy. And the next day . . .

. . . Vera sent a beautiful Christmas wreath to
Bianca by blackbird post. Mister Mole got
a wreath on top of his hill. And of course
Vera hung a wreath on her own front door.
Even Fritzy got a wreath. He tied it to his
ladder. Wrennie also got one for her nest. She
braided some pearls into hers, and Sara helped
her with the stars.

Vera washed her curtains for Christmas, but they weren't dry yet.

"I'm starting to feel gloomy looking at all those black holes," she said.

"Why don't you just look the other way?" said Dolly.

But Fritzy had a better idea. He cut out some stars, a moon, and a cloud. Mister Mole helped him hang them from the curtain rod. Suddenly the window looked very cheerful.

"That gives me an idea!" said Dolly. "Let's make a Christmas star. I'll glue some wrapping paper onto cardboard. Then I'll cut out a star."

"I'll paint little Sara on it!" shouted Fritzy.

"Then we can hang it up with a ribbon," said Dolly.

CHRISTMAS DOUGH ORNAMENTS

Vera loved her Christmas tree. And this year she had a new recipe for ornaments. Everyone came to help make them.

First Vera preheated the oven to 250° F. Then she mixed the salt, flour, and water together until a dough was formed.

Fritzy sprinkled a little flour on the countertop. Then he kneaded the dough on the floured surface until it was smooth and elastic.

Dolly dusted a rolling pin with flour. Then Vera rolled out the dough until it was about ¼ inch thick. Everyone wanted to help cut out the stars and moons and wreaths.

Fritzy's very favorite thing to do was punch the holes. Using a plastic straw, he poked a hole through each ornament.

Finally Vera put the ornaments on an ungreased baking sheet and baked them for 2 hours. When they had cooled completely, everyone helped put the ribbons through the holes and hang the ornaments on the tree. Sara thought they looked good enough to eat, but they did not taste good at all.

"Next year, let's paint them and sprinkle them with glitter," suggested Dolly.

"What a good idea!" said Vera.

A Christmas Cracker for Everyone!

When Vera sets the Christmas dinner table, she likes to put a Christmas cracker next to every plate. She and Sara and Dolly have so much fun making and filling the crackers. They can hardly wait until the guests arrive.

THIS IS WHAT YOU NEED:
toilet paper tubes
crepe paper
ribbon
small candies, toys, and messages for gifts
confetti
stickers and stars for decoration

 Cut a toilet paper tube into two halves.

 With the two halves together, wrap the toilet tube in crepe paper, with about 2 inches hanging on each side.

 Gather the crepe paper at one end, twist it, and tie it with a ribbon close to the roll.

 Write out some messages on small bits of paper. You might write fortunes such as NEXT YEAR YOU WILL GET ALL As. Or jokes such as WHAT GOES OH-OH-OH? (ANSWER: SANTA WALKING BACKWARD) Or gifts such as THIS TICKET IS GOOD FOR ONE BACK RUB.

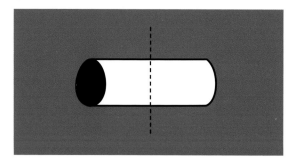

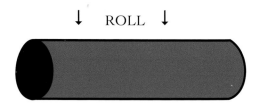

↓ ROLL ↓

Fill the tube with as many gifts, candies, and messages as you want. Spoon in some confetti.

 Gather the crepe paper on the other end of the roll, twist it, and tie it with a ribbon. [NOTE: Some crackers make a pop when you pull them apart. You can buy Christmas cracker bangers at many crafts shops. Just follow the directions on the package.]

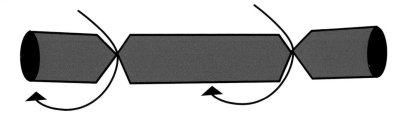

 Decorate your Christmas cracker with stickers and stars.

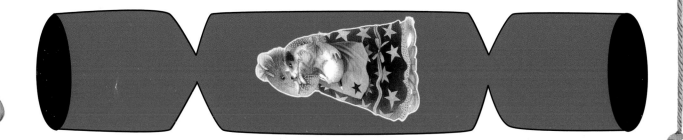

Christmas crackers were originally from England and are put next to the plates at dinner on Christmas evening.

As White As . . .

At last Bianca has arrived! Dolly was the first to see her.
With her white fur and her white coat, she wasn't easy to
spot in the white snow.

"Don't I look lovely all in white, Dolly?" said Bianca. "No owl will discover me in the snow. Camouflage, you see. Only an intelligent city mouse would think of that."

"Well, Bianca, you're not the only one to come up with that idea," said Dolly. That Bianca! She was really something else! "In the north, arctic hares are brown in the summer to blend in with the rocks and mud, but they turn white in the winter to blend in with the snow. And they don't need fancy clothes to do it."

"Ermines do that too," said Fritzy.

"Shhhh! Be quiet!" said Bianca. "Ermines *eat* mice!"

HOLLY

Vera had decorated the Christmas table with holly, but it didn't look so fresh anymore. Mr. Mole had spilled pudding on it. There was a blob right in the middle of it. And a little bird had been eating all the holly berries.

Christmas just won't be Christmas without holly, thought Vera. It was a good thing she knew where there was another bush.

The wheelbarrow was so full, there wasn't room for another berry.

"I wanted to ride home on the wheelbarrow," Fritzy moaned. "I'm so tired." He looked at Vera sadly. "I'm all tuckered out."

"Now Fritzy," said Vera. "You're a mouse in the prime of your life and you have strong, young legs. You have to help me push this wheelbarrow."

But Fritzy wasn't listening. He took a running jump right into the middle of the holly pile.

"OUCH!"

Vera couldn't help but laugh. "You shouldn't have done that, Fritzy," she said, chuckling.

Fritzy was laughing then too. "I guess not," he said, and they headed home with the holly, singing Christmas carols all the way.